T0198992

AuthorHouse™
1663 Liberty Drive
Bloomington, IN 47403
www.authorhouse.com
Phone: 1 (800) 839-8640

Published by AuthorHouse 12/18/2018

ISBN: 978-1-5462-7203-8 (sc)
ISBN: 978-1-5462-7202-1 (hc)
ISBN: 978-1-5462-7204-5 (e)

Library of Congress Control Number: 2018914649

Print information available on the last page.

This book is printed on acid-free paper.

authorHOUSE®

Grandma and Grandpa's Shorts

This book is lovingly dedicated to my grands:
Cruz, Yelitza, Camila and Johanna

Contents

Grandma's Apron

Every Sunday after church we go to Grandma's house for dinner. First, she goes to her pantry and pulls out a clean crisp apron. I asked her once why she had so many aprons and wore them almost all the time? "My Mother always wore one and gave me many over the years. They help save my dresses from splatters." She then got an apron out for Jo and me so we could be her helpers. She also showed us how she could use the corner of her apron to lift the lids on her pans to check her sauces or gravies on top of the stove. "I can open the oven on check on my casserole or cookies inside. I can also keep treats for you girls and Cruz when you visit. I can use the corner to wipe away tears when one you get hurt." I remember falling off the tire swing in the backyard and you did that for me Grandma!" Yes, I remember that I made it all better with a kiss on your cheek afterward. After dinner that Sunday Jo and I each left with two of Grandma's aprons that we could hardly wait to use.

Grandma's Fur Coat

*W*hen my Grandma died, I got her fur coat. I always loved to see her wear it on chilly Sunday mornings on our way to church or when she attended wedding or birthday celebrations with our family. I especially loved to see her it in her old picture albums. I love all those old pictures, but my favorite is the one of her about 20 years old at Christmas 1943 the day she got that beautiful fur coat. The pure joy in her eyes makes her look even more beautiful. Over the years, she took very loving care of that fur coat that would one day be mine. Excitedly hugging her fiancée as he returned safely from the war caused a huge rip where the sleeve is attached. Grandma told me this story over and over, I never interrupted her because I loved to hear this story so much. She said that she didn't fret about the big rip in her favorite coat. "My man returning home safely was so much more important." He sat and told me of his adventures in that far away land for some time while I stitched the inside and out of that coat. When I looked at the coat, I had to ask which sleeve was it Grandma? She had done such *an excellent job that I couldn't tell. Not so many years ago she joined her husband in heaven (the young soldier that she had hugged with such gusto that she ripped her coat). As she had agreed when she was gone her fur coat became mine. Sometimes my eyes tear with sadness when I look at her coat. Most times I joyfully add it to an outfit and impress my friends with how well it fits. They also comment on how much I remind them of Grandma when I wear it. My eyes well up with tears of happiness at those times as I agree.*

Grandmas Take a Cruise

Gammy and her cousin Glenda, we call her Auntie Glenda she is a Grandma too, anyway they went to Ft. Lauderdale... (that's in Florida) and got on a BIG cruise ship. I did not know it would be that big! Gammy said it was like a floating city. Sounds crazy that something that big would be able to float!

They spent the night with all of us at Jo's house. We went out to dinner and played in the pool until the fire flies were all around. All of us piled in the living room with Gammy and Auntie Glenda and told silly stories until we all fell asleep on our sleeping bags and blankets on the floor. After breakfast we drove to the Port of Ft. Lauderdale and Gammy and Auntie Glenda stood at the rail of the ship and waved at the babies Mila and Riena with Chris, Shaylee, Emmalyn, Yueles, Jo and me/Cruz until we could not tell if they were waving anymore or not and our moms said it was time to go.

Gammy said that they had a marvelous meal and made some new friends at the large dining table where they ate dinner. After that they found so many things to look at and take pictures. Familiar music was playing nearby so they followed the sound singing as they went. They find a piano player playing and singing songs from their youth. They sang loud along with others including the piano man. Auntie Glenda said that sometimes the piano man would stop singing and let the people around the piano sing. They heard more music being played loudly and there was a dance game going on Auntie Glenda joined in and Gammy made videos and took pictures.

There in the big auditorium was a stage where they watched a magician, comedians and lots of dancers with loads of feathers and sparkles on their costumes. Each night they slept like babies and could hardly wait for the next day and the adventures to start. The first morning they hung out around the pool and learned more about the ship and the fun things there were to do on it. Wave riders, rock climbers, jacuzzi lovers', swimmers, even ice skaters along with people eating and shopping all hours of the day and night. They went to four islands and brought us back lots of great souvenirs. Then Gammy leaned in close and said "Do you know what would make our next cruise even better? Jo, Yueles and I looked at each other not able to guess. "If all of you could come with us!" That made us all jump around our parents asking when we could go.

Grandma's Hair

My Abuela has beautiful long dark hair with no tangles or knots to be seen. It frames her face in an ebony sheen.

Gammy or Nono, as I renamed her when I was two, has had lots of lengths and colors of hair on her head. Now she is growing all that out and letting her grey and dark hair show.

At my school, my friend Devon has a grandma that has grey hair crawling out from under what Mommy tells me is a wig. She showed my sister and I some in the mall once. She also said not to talk about it to Devon's grandma because it might make her sad.

Kathy has a grandma that brings her to school, and she has a big braid wrapped round and round her head. Kathy says that when her Nana lets her hair down it is past her knees!

Quentin's grandma wears beautiful scarves and hats everywhere. Quentin says it is because his grandma had cancer and the medicines made all her hair fall out.

When my sister is a grandma I wonder what her hair will look like. Right now her hair is straight and in her eyes or in little ponytails that look a bit like water sprays coming out of her head!

My Mommy says that when women become Grandmothers they have earned the right to wear their hair anyway, anywhere they wish!

Introducing my very FIRST

Grandpa Short

I hope you love it!

Grandpa's Hands

*M*y Grandpa's hands may not look like anything special to you. But to me they are super special! I lived with my Grandpa and Grandma most of my life. Grandpa's hands held me when I was small. His hands fixed my broken toys. Those same hands kept me safe while I learned to ride my bike.

I watched my Grandpa's hands take apart my Grandma's car and put on new parts to make it work again. When Grandma's mixer stopped working, she was ready to go to the store and buy another. Grandpa said, "Hold on Georgia, give it to me". Within the hour he brought it back from his workshop working as good as new. It was the same with anything I can think of that ever broke in their house. I thought that there was nothing that my Grandpa's hands could not fix.

Once when we visited, he had dug a mountain of dirt out from under his house to make a cellar for Grandma's home canned foods. He made a huge wheel barrow to haul that dirt out. My cousins and me called it the "baby carriage" because that it looked more like that than a wheelbarrow to us. We would wheel each other around the yard in it. After hours of rolling around the yard, we became board. Well, we found out the hard way that rolling a cousin down the hill in front of Grandpa's house was not a good idea!

Grandma's Hair was compressed to accommodate this particular book. You can still order it in its entirety including, illustrations of all my grandmas online. Just go to Amazon.com or BarnesandNobles.com.

Printed in the United States
By Bookmasters